I'M HOT

Leon

by Cécile Gagnon
Illustrated by Darcia Labrosse

Translated from the French by Patricia Claxton

M&S

for Françoise, Mathieu
and Jehoshùa

J'AI CHAUD
Original edition
© Les éditions du Raton Laveur, 1986

I'M HOT
Translation by Patricia Claxton
Copyright © by McClelland and Stewart, 1988

All rights reserved. The use of any part of this publication,
reproduced, transmitted in any form or by any means,
electronic, mechanical, photocopying, recording, or otherwise,
or stored in a retrieval system, without the prior consent of
the publisher is an infringement of the copyright law.

This translation was completed with the assistance of
the Canada Council.

Canadian Cataloguing in Publication Data

Gagnon, Cécile, 1938-
    (J'ai chaud. English)
    I'm hot

Translation of: J'ai chaud.
ISBN 0-7710-3284-6 (bound) 0-7710-3288-9 (pkt.)

I. Labrosse, Darcia. II. Title. III. Title:
J'ai chaud. English.

PS8513.A345J3413 1988 jC843'.54 C88-094349-1
PZ10.3.G33lm 1988

Typeset by VictoR GAD studio
Printed and bound in Canada

McClelland and Stewart
The Canadian Publishers
481 University Avenue
Toronto, Ontario
M5G 2E9

After a long voyage on an iceberg, Leon had come to the land of trees.
He heard a rustling sound close by.

"Hi!" said Alex the raccoon.

"Uh . . . hello," said Leon, surprised and happy to meet someone. "It smells good here."

"It's summer and there are lots of flowers," said Alex. "Here, smell some."

"This one doesn't smell at all," said Leon, "but how pretty it is!"

Alex and Leon had fun in the woods together. They ran, they jumped, they climbed, they kicked their feet in the air.

But when the sun shone through the leaves at noon, Leon flopped at the foot of a big oak tree.

"I'm hot, I'm hot!"

Alex looked at him and said, "Your fur's too long."

"I'm hot," said Leon again. "Much too hot."

"I'll cut your fur for you," said Alex, "and then you'll feel cooler."

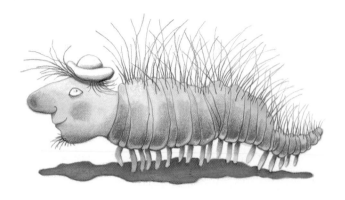

Leon sat on a tree stump.
Alex took a pair of scissors and began to cut. Snip, snip, snip.
The white fur fell softly to the ground.
Leon was feeling better already.

When the job was done, Leon stood up.
"How light I am!" he said. "I don't feel hot
at all any more."

Suddenly, hundreds of birds flew down, cheeping and cawing. They were very excited. The news had spread from beak to beak.

"There's something new to build with."

"Just when we need it most."

"I've already begun to build."

"Leave some for me!"

By nightfall there was not a single tuft
of fur left on the ground.
The birds had cleaned it all up.

" Thank you, Leon, thank you."
"Our nests are warm . . . "
" . . . and so-o-o comfortable!"

The moon couldn't believe her eyes.
In the woods that year all the nests
were white.

Cécile Gagnon has produced over forty books for children and young adults, several of which have received prestigious awards. Her ability to capture the language, rhythms and understanding of children has been internationally recognized. She received the Province of Quebec Prize in 1970, and the ACELF children's literature prize in 1980 and 1985. Until recently she was editor-in-chief of *Coulicou* in Montreal, the French version of *Chickadee* magazine for children.

Darcia Labrosse wrote and illustrated her first children's book when she was seventeen. It was published nine years later, along with her first collaboration with Cécile Gagnon. She is also a prize-winning film animator and painter. In 1983 she received the Canada Council prize for children's illustration, and in 1987 she received the Governor General's Award for *Welcome to the World*.

Patricia Claxton is a highly regarded translator living in Montreal. Most recently she translated Gabrielle Roy's autobiography, *Enchantment and Sorrow*, for which she received the 1987 Governor General's Award.